Published in the United States by Clarkson N. Potter, Inc., One Park Avenue,
New York, New York 10016 and simultaneously in Canada by General Publishing
Company Limited.

Clarkson N. Potter, Potter, and colophon are trademarks of Clarkson N. Potter, Inc.

Published in Great Britain by Aurum Press Ltd., 33 Museum Street,
London WC1A 1LD, England

Manufactured in Belgium by Henri Proost & CIE PVBA

Library of Congress Cataloging in Publication Data

Holabird, Katharine.
    Angelina at the fair.

    Summary: Angelina's annoyance at having to take her
little Cousin Henry to the fair turns into friendship
after a day filled with adventures and surprises.
    1. Children's stories, English. (1. Fairs – Fiction.
2. Cousins – Fiction) I. Craig, Helen, ill. II. Title.
PZ7.H689Aq 1985   (E)   84-28931
ISBN 0-517-55744-4

10 9 8 7 6 5 4 3 2 1

First Edition

Angelina at the Fair

Illustrations by Helen Craig Story by Katharine Holabird

Clarkson N. Potter, Inc./Publishers NEW YORK
DISTRIBUTED BY CROWN PUBLISHERS, INC.

All winter long Angelina had been saving her pennies for the wonderful day when the fair would come again. When she wasn't busy dancing, she would sit by her window and daydream about the ferris wheels and roller coasters. She liked all the most exciting rides.

At last, when all the snow had melted, and the wind was soft and warm again, the May Day Fair arrived in town. Angelina's ballet class performed a maypole dance at school in celebration of spring, and Angelina almost flew around the maypole she was so excited. All the parents watched and cheered.

After the dance Angelina was ready to go to the fair
with her friends, but her parents stopped her. "You've
forgotten that little cousin Henry is visiting today," said
Angelina's father. "He will be very disappointed if he
can't go to the fair with you."

Angelina was furious. "I don't want to take Henry!" she
said. "I hate little boys!" But Henry held out his hand
just the same, and Angelina had to take him with her.
The music from the fair was already floating across the
fields, and Angelina's friends had gone ahead. She
grabbed Henry's hand and dragged him along behind
her, running as fast as she could.

At the entrance to the fair was a stand of brightly colored balloons. "Oh, look!" cried Henry. "Balloons!"

But Angelina didn't pay any attention. "We're going on the ferris wheel," she said. The ferris wheel was huge and Henry was frightened, but Angelina loved the feeling of soaring up in the air and so they took two rides.

When they got off Henry felt sick, but he cheered up when he saw the merry-go-round. "Look!" he said, smiling. "Can we go on that?" "Not now," said Angelina. "We're going on the fast rides." She took poor Henry on the roller coaster. Henry shut his eyes and held on tightly as the little car zoomed up and down the tracks. Angelina loved it and wanted to go again, but Henry wasn't sure he wanted to take any more rides at all.

Then Angelina saw the Haunted House.
"You'll like this," she said, and pulled Henry inside.

A big spider dangled just above their heads as they went in . . .

and a skeleton jumped out and pointed right at them.

When they bumped into a ghost
Angelina reached out to touch Henry. . .

but he was gone!

"Henry, Henry," Angelina called, but there was no answer in the darkness. Angelina hurried back through the Haunted House trying to find him.

She looked everywhere until she got tangled up in the
spider and had to be rescued by the ticket seller.

Angelina didn't see Henry outside the Haunted House, either. She ran through the crowds looking for him. She ran past all the rides and all the games, but Henry was nowhere to be found. At last she was so worried and upset that she sat down by the entrance to the fair and began to cry.

And there, watching the balloon man blow up the beautiful balloons, was Henry! Angelina was so relieved that she gave him a big hug and a kiss. "What is your favorite color, Henry?" she asked. Henry chose a blue balloon.

"What would you like to do now?" Angelina asked kindly.

Henry said he would like to go on the merry-go-round,

so they went three times, and they both loved it.

Afterward they had a double chocolate ice-cream cone
and walked home slowly together. "I like fairs," said
Henry, and Angelina smiled.
"You can come with me anytime," she said.